The Fox and the Kingfisher

written by JUDITH MELLECKER

illustrated by ROBERT ANDREW PARKER

ALFRED A. KNOPF · NEW YORK

THIS IS A BORZOI BOOK
PUBLISHED BY ALFRED A. KNOPF, INC.

Text copyright © 1990 by Judith Mellecker
Illustrations copyright © 1990 by Robert Andrew Parker
All rights reserved under International and Pan-American Copyright
Conventions. Published in the United States by Alfred A. Knopf, Inc.,
New York, and simultaneously in Canada by Random House of Canada
Limited, Toronto. Distributed by Random House, Inc., New York.
Book design by Elizabeth Hardie
Manufactured in Singapore

2 4 6 8 0 9 7 5 3 1

Library of Congress Cataloging-in-Publication Data
Mellecker, Judith. The fox and the kingfisher /
by Judith Mellecker ; illustrated by Robert Andrew Parker. p. cm.
Summary: Unhappy with their father's plan to remarry,
a brother and sister have their wishes fulfilled by a
stableboy who knows magic and are turned into
a fox and a kingfisher.
ISBN 0-679-80539-7.—ISBN 0-679-90539-1 (lib. bdg.)
[1. Magic—Fiction. 2. Animals—Fiction.
3. Brothers and sisters—Fiction. 4. Remarriage—Fiction.]
I. Parker, Robert Andrew, ill. II. Title.
PZ7.M515975Fo 1990 [E]—dc20 89-27180

For my parents
—J. M.

For my grandparents,
who were Will and Julia Cowdin
—R. A. P.

In the early years of this century Captain John Reynolds and his son and daughter, Desmond and Daisy, lived in a large stone house near the village of Burne, in county Durham in the north of England. In summer the broad fields around the house were white with sheep grazing amid the wildflowers. In autumn the land turned purple and brown as the farmers began their harvest. At Christmastime, Desmond and Daisy would gather evergreen boughs for holiday decorations. The captain and his family had known much happiness together, but in recent years the beautiful house in which they lived had become a lonely place. A voice—a presence—was gone. In 1902, during an outbreak of influenza, the children's mother had died.

One year, a few days before Christmas, Captain Reynolds had a huge pine tree cut down in the forest and carried into the drawing room. There it stood, dark green and magnificent, its needles cold and dusted with snow. Desmond and Daisy carefully placed gold ornaments on the tree. Their mother had made the ornaments herself, when she was a little girl. The captain looked at his children kindly. He loved them very much and hoped that what he was about to say would make them happy.

"Children," he said, "I have an announcement, a Christmas present for all of us." Desmond and Daisy stood quietly. Before their mother had died, they had been high-spirited creatures, playful as little goats. But now they were often sad and silent, and far too obedient. "Children, Miss Penney and I are going to be married." Miss Penney was a pretty lady who lived across the valley, in Minton. Desmond and Daisy scarcely knew her. One afternoon they had all had tea together. But they knew that their father visited her. He would often ride over to Minton on his chestnut mare—the mare whose shining red coat made Desmond think of his mother's hair.

Though Desmond and Daisy were stunned by their father's announcement, they listened politely and said nothing. Desmond turned very pale.

Later the children went outside to collect pine cones. Down by the stable Daisy at last began to cry. "No!" she said. "I don't want her here."

Desmond tried to comfort her. "It's all right, Daisy," he said, holding back his own tears. "We'll stay up in our rooms all day long. Father has Miss Penney now. He won't mind." But he disbelieved his own words.

The new stableboy, a lad named Firr, listened nearby. Firr was small and thin, with a thatch of dark hair and brown arms as strong as the leather tack the horses wore. No one knew where he had come from, but everyone saw that Firr was a wizard with animals. His hand on a horse's neck soothed the beast like a motherly caress on a child's brow. With Firr close by, the stable dogs stopped quarreling and peacefully shared their scraps of meat and bone. Firr could make a butterfly land on a cat's ear, and he could make a cat smile.

Firr never spoke to the adults, but he was not afraid of Desmond and Daisy. When he saw how unhappy they were, he asked, "Master Desmond? Miss Daisy? Whatever is the matter? Come inside where it's warm, and tell me."

"Oh!" cried Daisy. "Father is going to marry Miss Penney. I wish I could fly away!" Daisy liked to be dramatic.

Desmond, speaking rudely of Miss Penney, said, "I hate her. I'd rather live in a hole than stay here."

Firr thought for a moment. In his eyes the children were like the animals in his care: they were helpless, and they needed him. "Well, then," he murmured. He lifted a gold key from a hook on the wall and said, "This is a wishing key. It is older than the stones under your feet." The key glowed in Firr's hand. "You're quite sure, now, Miss Daisy?" he said. "You'd like to fly away?"

"Oh, yes!" she said.

Firr tapped the key three times on Daisy's head. He stamped his foot three times. Daisy vanished.

"Oh!" gasped Desmond. A kingfisher fluttered around his head, chirping wildly.

"That's your young sister, I believe," Firr said modestly. Desmond laughed.

Firr tapped the key on Desmond's head, then stamped his foot. Before the boy had a chance to blink, he turned into a fox.

The fox streaked off, followed by the wildly chirping kingfisher.

"Be happy," Firr commanded.

That first night the fox and the kingfisher traveled deep into the forest. The woods were dark and cold and full of a listening silence—as though the trees had ears and could hear every sound that was made. If Desmond had been a little boy, he would have wanted to be safe in his cozy bed. But because he was a fox, he found a hollow at the base of a tree, curled his tail around himself, and fell asleep. He was very tired.

Daisy rested in the branches overhead. Dinner had been a few grubs and water insects she had found in an icy stream. At home, she would have had chicken stew and raspberry trifle for dessert—one of her favorite meals. But now that she was enchanted and had been turned into a bird, the water insects were almost as delicious as chicken and raspberries. "Good night, good night," she chirped happily to the fox. "Aren't we lucky?"

Captain Reynolds was distraught when he learned the children were missing. Where could they be? Had they run away? He realized that the announcement of his marriage to Miss Penney had upset them. This made him sad, because he knew that Miss Penney—his dear Miranda—would be a kind and loving mother to the children.

The captain and his friends and neighbors formed search parties and looked everywhere for Desmond and Daisy. They scoured the local villages and tramped the fields. Out in the stable Firr stayed among the horses and said nothing. He worked hard, ate his food, and slept in the straw. He kept his silence.

On Christmas Eve the chief of the Burne Constabulary was escorted into the receiving hall. He had unhappy news for Captain Reynolds. "I'm so sorry, sir," he said. "There has not been a trace of the youngsters."

It was a melancholy Christmas, even though every corner of the great stone house was decorated with spruce and juniper boughs, sprigs of holly and mistletoe, and wreaths of pine. There was the fragrance of plum pudding and roast beef and ginger cookies. There were baskets of nuts and pears, and piles of bright packages under the Christmas tree. Captain Reynolds gave Miss Penney a silver locket inscribed with her name. Miss Penney gave the captain a watch fob inscribed with his initials.

As the days went by, the winter turned colder. The wind howled across the dry fields and blew snow deep into the forest where the fox and the kingfisher lived. The fox's coat grew thick and warm. He chased rabbits and hunted for voles and mice. The kingfisher remained hidden in the trees. "Tweetle, tweetle," she chirped. When she perched on a branch and let the sun warm her feathers, the fox was close by, alert and protective. And in the language that animals have—and human beings can only wonder about—they would sometimes talk to each other.

The wedding of Miss Penney and Captain Reynolds took place in the Great Hall. Miss Penney wore a white dress of silk and lace and a sprig of holly in her dark hair. Captain Reynolds, who had served with distinction in several campaigns, wore the dress uniform of the Durham Light Infantry. He looked very handsome.

Two places remained empty at the banquet table, for Captain and Mrs. Reynolds continued to hope for the return of Desmond and Daisy.

One day the kingfisher heard dogs barking. She flew to the top of a tree and saw a pack of hounds off in the distance. It was a fox hunt. She chirped frantically and flew down to the fox. "Fly! Fly!" she cried.

The fox was resting after a tasty meal of dried apples and voles. He rolled over onto his back and batted his paws. He wanted to play. "Run for your life!" the kingfisher warned him. "The hounds are coming this way!"

The fox looked bewildered. His expression was the same as Desmond's when he was asked a difficult mathematics question. Then an instant later the fox dashed away.

The kingfisher flew overhead. She could see the riders' red jackets and hear the crack of their whips. The hunting horn sounded: "Ta-raah!"

The fox, terrified and confused, began to run in a circle. "No, no!" exclaimed the kingfisher. "Not that way. Go through the pine grove and down to the fields. Hurry!"

The fox raced through the dried grass. He could hear the hunt behind him—the yips and cries of the hounds, the pounding of the horses' hooves. He ran and ran, and the harder he ran, the more he wished to be a boy again.

Then at last the cries faded away. The fox trotted to a knoll overlooking a quiet field. The kingfisher fluttered about his head. "Look!" she said. "It's the farm!" Across the field and beyond a stand of trees they could see the stone house. "Oh, I miss it so!" said the kingfisher. "I want to see Father. And I want to see my room again. My yellow room."

The fox said sadly, "They won't take us in, you know. Father wouldn't allow us in his house." He sighed in despair. "I don't think he would recognize you, and he certainly would not know me."

The kingfisher ignored him. "I want to go back, Desmond."

They waited in the field until it was dark. The moon rose and was so bright that the fox cast a shadow as he trotted in the direction of the house. The kingfisher darted about and found an open window by the kitchen door. The fox jumped inside and at that moment felt joy and fear, for he remembered that the house dogs would be sleeping by the fireplace in the drawing room. Silently the fox and the kingfisher moved through the halls and across the dining room with its huge polished table and silver bowl shining in the gloom. As he padded down the hall to the library, the fox heard the dogs growl in their sleep.

In a corner of the library was a pile of gaily wrapped boxes. Their presents from Christmas! The kingfisher and the fox pecked and clawed at the bright wrappings just as if it were Christmas morning. The dogs growled again and thumped their heavy tails on the floor. The intruders fled from the house.

All that winter Captain Reynolds and Miranda kept their vigil. And though the search continued for the children, people in the district were beginning to think of other things. Winter was ending. It was lambing season and soon would be time for spring planting. As the days grew warmer, the captain and Miranda took long walks through the grounds. Miranda had grown to love the beautiful stone house and her new life with the captain. But she, too, needed Desmond and Daisy there to make it perfect.

The household had quickly learned that someone—or something—had torn open the Christmas presents. On an afternoon walk the captain and Miranda discussed this puzzling event. When they reached the stable, they looked in on a newborn foal. "How I wish Desmond and Daisy were here to see this small creature," said Miranda. The captain nodded sadly in agreement.

Firr stood close by, listening. He was still just a boy and did not know what to believe about the world or the magic powers of the key. But he as well longed for the children.

After Captain and Mrs. Reynolds left the stable, Firr went outside. The air smelled of turned-over earth and damp grass. As the afternoon light began to fade, blue shadows appeared on the grass. It grew very still, as though life itself had stopped. Firr waited. A shadow began to move his way—a small shadow with paws and a pointed face. It was the fox. Firr looked down at him and said, "Aye, sir. I know you. I was hoping you'd be back."

The fox lifted his face to Firr. His eyes were dark, glittering, and held a purely human expression of yearning and sorrow. Firr offered his hand. The fox pushed at it with his muzzle.

Firr spoke again. "I believe I know why you're here." He took the gold key from around his neck. "You've been gone so long a time, sir. We've missed you terribly." Firr lightly tapped the key on the fox's head, right between his ears. Then Firr stamped the ground three times.

Nothing happened. Firr stamped the ground again, harder. The fox vanished, and in his place stood Desmond, his clothes ragged and dirty, looking at once startled and miserable. Then he laughed. "Firr!" he shouted. "You did it! Daisy!" The kingfisher swooped down from the stable roof. Firr repeated his magic. He tapped the key and stamped the ground. The kingfisher disappeared in a little cloud of dust and feathers. Daisy stood before them, her dress streaked with mud, and with pine needles and bits of bark in her hair. "Hurrah!" she cried. Desmond and Daisy hugged Firr and then ran off toward the house.

Firr waited a moment and then slowly drew back his thin, strong right arm. The powers of the wishing key were too strange and frightening. He wanted no more of magic. He flung the key high into the sky. It soared in an arc, caught the light of the sun, and then tumbled to earth, disappearing from view.

The captain and Miranda were sitting in the garden, surrounded by the light green haze of plants just coming into leaf, when they noticed that the bushes and flowers began to grow. Buds ripened and blossomed before their very eyes.

Then they heard footsteps running up the path. Desmond and Daisy appeared by the garden wall, pink-faced and breathless, their clothes in tatters. The captain was almost speechless, but managed to say "Oh, thank heaven!" before embracing his children.

Desmond, not used to speaking in a quiet human voice, shouted, "We lived in the forest, Father! But we love you! We had to come back!"

Daisy shyly took Miranda's hand and asked, "Will we be friends?"

Miranda smiled and said, "Oh, my, yes. Good friends."

Desmond leaned against Captain Reynolds's shoulder and gazed at Miranda's radiant face. "We have so much to tell you and Father!" he exclaimed.

"Yes, we do," said Daisy. "And we're so happy to be home."

Judith Mellecker, a writer and editor, was on the staff of *The New Yorker* for many years and was a contributor to the Talk of the Town department. *The Fox and the Kingfisher* is her first book for children. She lives in New York City.

Robert Andrew Parker, a Caldecott Honor winner and Guggenheim Fellow, has twice been selected by *The New York Times Book Review* for a Best Illustrated Children's Book of the Year award. His work is in the collections of museums across the country, including New York's MOMA, the Whitney Museum of American Art, and the Metropolitan Museum of Art. He teaches at the Parsons School of Design and lives in West Cornwall, Connecticut.